It was a nice summer day in the country. The sun was warm. Birds were singing. But instead of enjoying everything, I was holding my breath. Scared stiff!

Seeing the man in the cemetery was what shook me up. He was tall and very thin. His hair slicked back, the old wet look. He had black eyes. A nose that curved down like a bird's beak. His face white as chalk. He was wearing a black suit. He was standing near the tombstones in the graveyard.

Dracula! I knew he was Dracula the moment I saw him.

KIN PLATT was born in New York City and is currently living in Los Angeles. He is a well-known author of books that deal directly with contemporary problems: *The Boy Who Could Make Himself Disappear; Chloris and the Creeps; Headman; Hey, Dummy;* and *Run for Your Life.* He is also the author of *Mystery of the Witch Who Wouldn't.* These are all available in Laurel-Leaf editions.

LAUREL-LEAF BOOKS bring together under a single imprint outstanding works of fiction and nonfiction particularly suitable for young adult readers, both in and out of the classroom. Charles F. Reasoner, Professor of Elementary Education, New York University, is the consultant to this series.

BY KIN PLATT

DRACULA, GO HOME!

Illustrations by
Frank Mayo

Published by
Dell Publishing Co., Inc.
1 Dag Hammarskjold Plaza
New York, New York 10017

Text copyright © 1979 by Kin Platt
Illustrations copyright © 1979 by Franklin Watts, Inc.

Laurel-Leaf Library ® TM 766734, Dell Publishing Co., Inc.

ISBN: 0-440-92022-1

RL: 2.4

Reprinted by arrangement with Franklin Watts, Inc.

Printed in the United States of America

First Laurel-Leaf printing—February 1981

DRACULA, GO HOME!

CHAPTER

It was a nice summer day in the country. The sun was warm. Birds were singing. But instead of enjoying everything, I was holding my breath. Scared stiff!

Seeing the man in the cemetery was what shook me up. He was tall and very thin. His hair was slicked back, the old wet look. He had black eyes. A nose that curved down like a bird's beak. His face white as chalk. He was wearing a black suit. He was standing near the tombstones in the graveyard.

Dracula! I knew he was Dracula the moment I saw him.

I was taking a shortcut from the station in a town called Hammond. It was summer vacation and I was going to spend it with my Aunt Shirley. She owned an old hotel. My folks had an idea I could help out there.

The train came in late and nobody was there to meet me. Some people in town gave me directions. I got lost on the way and had to cut through the cemetery. If I hadn't seen Dracula there, I might have had a terrific vacation.

It's too crazy, I told myself first. But though I was new to the town of Hammond, I knew Dracula when I saw him. I'd seen him in TV movies plenty of times. The man who lives forever. The vampire.

A vampire is something you can live without. It is a corpse that comes to life after midnight. It flies like a giant bat and sucks the blood of sleeping people. After it bites you on the neck and takes your blood, you become its slave.

If the stories are true, the vampire Dracula has been living over a thousand years.

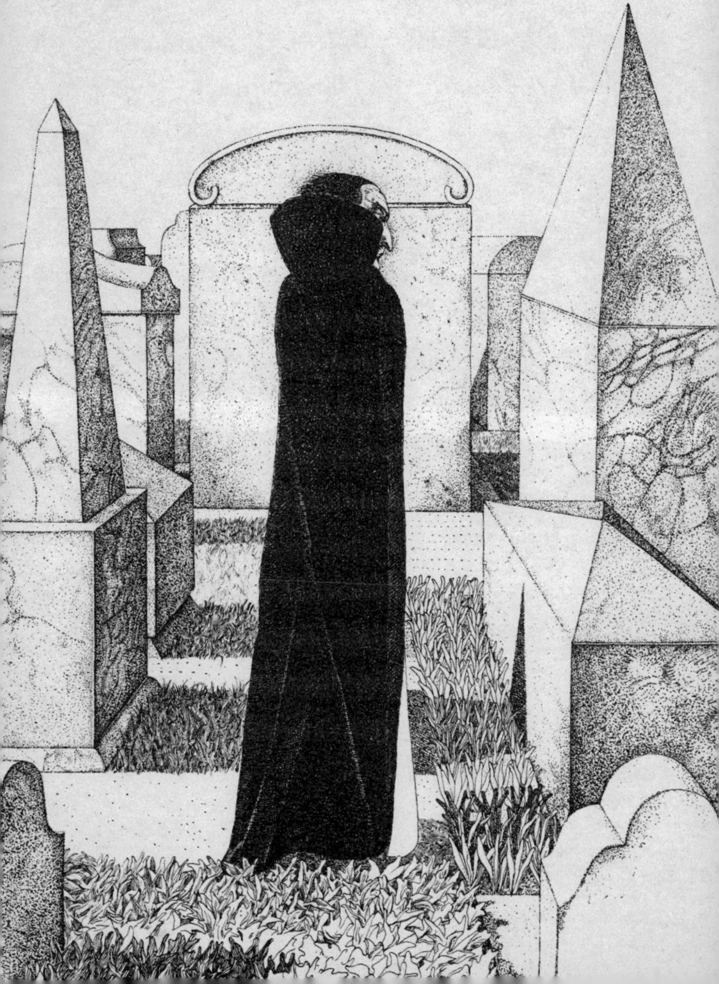

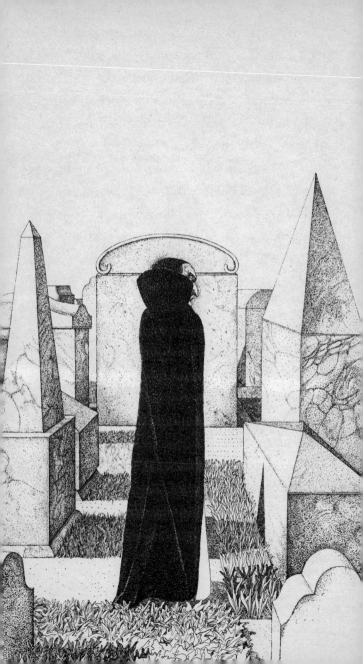

I stood rooted, afraid to move. His back was now turned toward me and he was looking around at the tombstones. What's he doing? I asked myself. Vampires are supposed to sleep during the day. If he's Dracula, he's supposed to be in his coffin. The sun was still up.

Behind the white tombstones was a big marble vault. The kind that has the underground burial chambers. The coffin for him to be sleeping in would be somewhere at the bottom.

But instead of being asleep in there, here he was out in the open at midday. Breaking the vampire rules. Maybe it got too hot for him to sleep, I told myself. I didn't know very much about vampires and their sleeping habits. Only what I remembered from the TV movies.

Then I had an idea that made me feel better. Maybe he's not Dracula, after all, dummy. He's a man who just happens to look like him.

I began to back away. A dry twig snapped as I stepped on it. The tall thin man turned and saw me.

His lips twisted in a snarl. I saw white teeth. His black eyes glittered under dark frowning brows. They bored into mine from ten yards away as if they were laser beams. I felt drained from the power in his eyes. My knees got weak.

I backed off into the trees. My suitcase felt like it was full of bricks. In my hurry to get away, I slipped and tripped. I was sweating when I found the main road.

I kept hurrying until I got to my aunt's old hotel. Before I ran up the steps, I looked around. He wasn't following me.

I only felt that he was.

CHAPTER

My Aunt Shirley is my mom's sister. Her husband, my Uncle Bob, was killed in a hunting accident a few years ago. Since then, she has had to run the big old hotel by herself.

"I'm glad you could make it, Larry," my aunt said. "We can use a strong busboy."

What happened to my dream of running the hotel, I wondered.

"How about waiting on table?" I asked.

My aunt shook her head. "Sorry, Jill Baker has that job. She's in high school, too, like you. You'll meet her at dinner tonight. You'll like Jill."

Then she showed me around. It was a big white clapboard building. There were tall oaks over a hundred years old all around the front grounds. So the hotel was called The Oaks.

The main floor had the dining room, kitchen, and TV room. The TV room had a Ping-Pong table, too. A wide porch at the front had old wicker chairs, rockers and a sofa. The desk in the front hall for signing in guests was high, the wood worn and polished.

There were thirty rooms. Fifteen on the first floor up. Another fifteen on the next floor up.

My aunt opened a door. "I'm putting you in here, Larry. Number twelve. It has a nice view of the mountains."

I left my bag and we went downstairs. She showed me how to check guests in and out. How to handle the money. Where the keys were. She showed me the linen closet with the towels, sheets, and pillowcases.

"In case I'm out, you'll have to handle things," she said.

"Swell," I said.

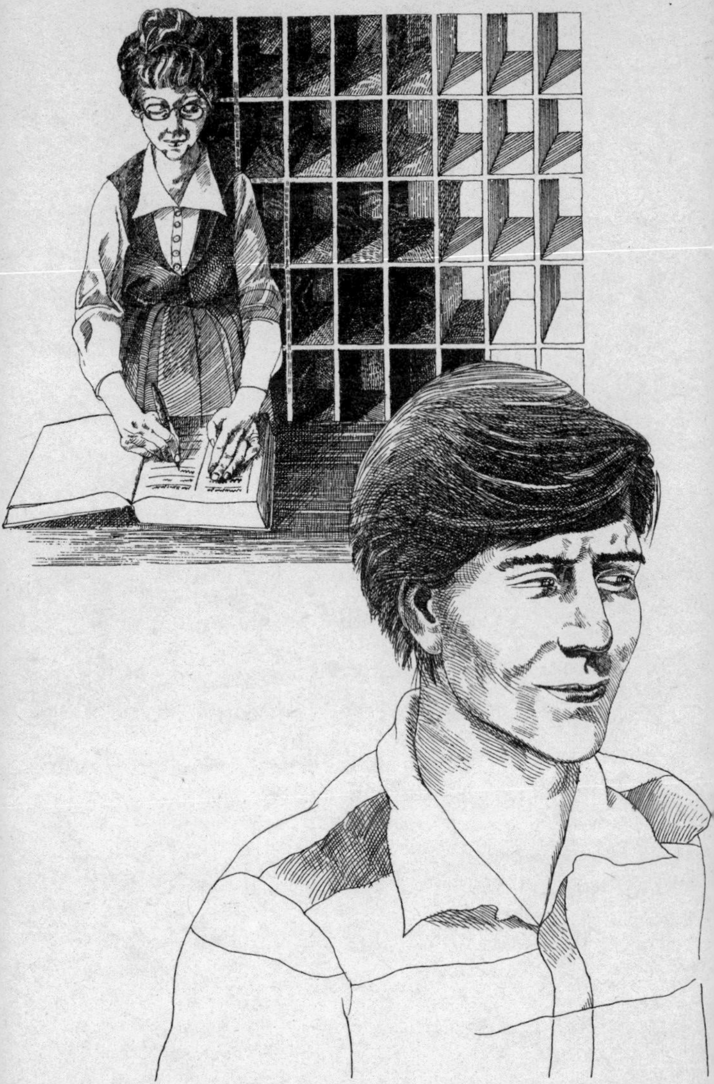

"We have a big lake. When you have any free time, you can go swimming."

I asked what else was around to do.

"Not very much," she said. "There's a movie house in town and a library. Or you can watch TV here. Nothing much ever happens in Hammond."

She didn't know it then, but she was all wrong about that.

CHAPTER

3

Jill Baker said everything with a smile. "Hi, my name is Jill," she said.

Instead of saying I was crazy about her right off, I said, "I'm Larry Carter. I came up here to help my aunt run this hotel on my summer vacation."

"Well, me, too," she said. "But I also need the bread for college. I'm saving up."

"Good idea. I'll need to do that, too."

"I'm glad you came," Jill said. "So far I've been waiting on table and also clearing away the dishes. I've been dreaming of a busboy."

"Well, okay, now you got one."

"Terrific. Have you worked in a hotel before?"

"First time," I said.

"It's no big deal. The hotel is only half full now. By the time it fills up, you won't be dropping any more dishes."

"How soon will that be?" I asked.

"Next week. There's a good summer theater in town. And people come from all over to see the shows. A lot of them will stop off here at your aunt's hotel. She serves good food."

"Maybe we can go to one of the shows some time," I said.

Jill lost her smile. "I don't know how. They start at 7:30 while we're in the middle of serving dinner."

"Oh," I said. "Well, maybe my aunt will give us a night off. I dig shows."

"You do? Terrific. Maybe you'll be seeing me in one someday."

I stared. "No kidding? You going to be an actress?"

"You better believe it. I'm with the theater group at school now. We've done six plays so far."

"I bet you're good," I said.

She tossed her hair back, smiling. "I just knew I was going to like the new busboy."

I was grinning about that when my aunt called me. The cook had cut his hand. He needed somebody to peel the potatoes.

That's how it goes in the hotel business.

CHAPTER

The next day I was kept busy. The dishwasher was sick. I scrubbed and washed about a million pots, pans, and dishes.

My aunt had to do some shopping in town. I took over at the desk. Two new people came in for rooms. I had them sign the register book. I helped bring up their bags. I told them what time meals were served and so on.

Two people checked out. I gave them their bills. One wrote out a check. The other gave me his credit card. Nobody uses money anymore.

Then it was time for lunch. I was a busboy again.

I was so busy I forgot all about the man who looked like Dracula.

At times, Jill helped out, too. Together we could clean and shape up a room in half the time. Working together made the job more fun.

It was after lunch the second day. Aunt Shirley had gone to the bank in the village. I told her to take her time. I could run the hotel myself for a few hours.

I was sitting behind the front desk. Reading a book. Suddenly I had a tingling feeling. I felt that somebody was standing real close, watching me. So I looked up.

There he was. Dracula.

I never heard him come in.

I never saw him until he was right there.

His face was even whiter than it was in the graveyard.

I gulped. That means he's fresh out of blood, I thought.

He was bigger and looked more powerful

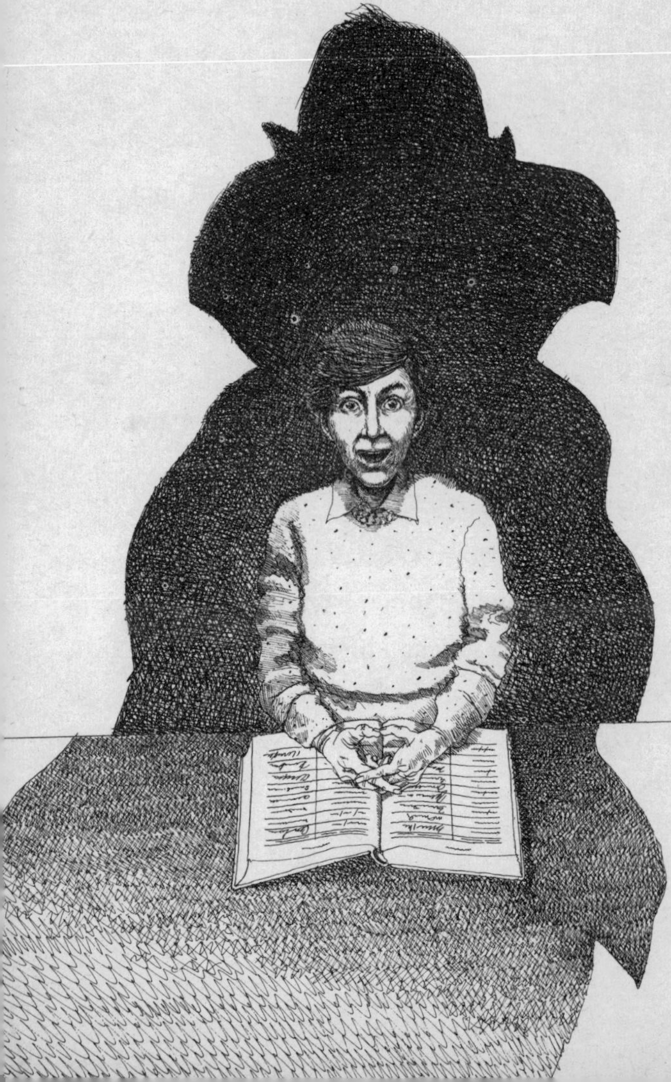

than I remembered. His voice was deep. "Young man, may I trouble you for a room?"

I stood up fast. My heart began to thump. Cool it, you dope, I told myself. If he wants a room, then he can't be Dracula. Vampires don't spend money to sleep in hotels. They use graveyards.

I couldn't tell if he recognized me. He was wearing a hat now. Pulled down low and shading his eyes. Not many people wear hats. Hardly any in the summer.

Did vampires wear hats? I didn't know.

I pushed the registry book toward him. "Yes, sir. Will you sign in, please? And do you know how long you will be staying?"

He took the pen and began writing in the book. There are three spaces on the page. Name, city, and state. The book was upside down from me as he wrote. I didn't try to read it.

"Is Room 13 available?" he said. "I've been here before and I like the view."

I had kept up with what rooms were empty or occupied. "Yes, sir. That's the big double room. Fifteen dollars a day."

"Fine," he said. "I'll be staying for a few days."

"Swell." I turned the book toward me to read his name. The handwriting was small and neat, and straight up and down.

A. R. Claud. Belgrade

My voice sounded weak. "All right, Mr. Claud. If you'll follow me. I'll help you up with your bag."

He shook his head slowly. His black eyes bored into mine. All of a sudden, I didn't feel like moving. "No need to trouble you, my boy. My bag is light and I know my way to the room. If you'll just hand me the key, please."

I gave him the key. Dropped it on the desk and saw his white hand pick it up. Don't be nervous, I told myself.

"Breakfast is at seven," I said. "Lunch at twelve. Dinner starts at six."

He was moving away. "Yes, I know."

He seemed to glide up the steps. He turned out of sight at the landing. His footsteps faded

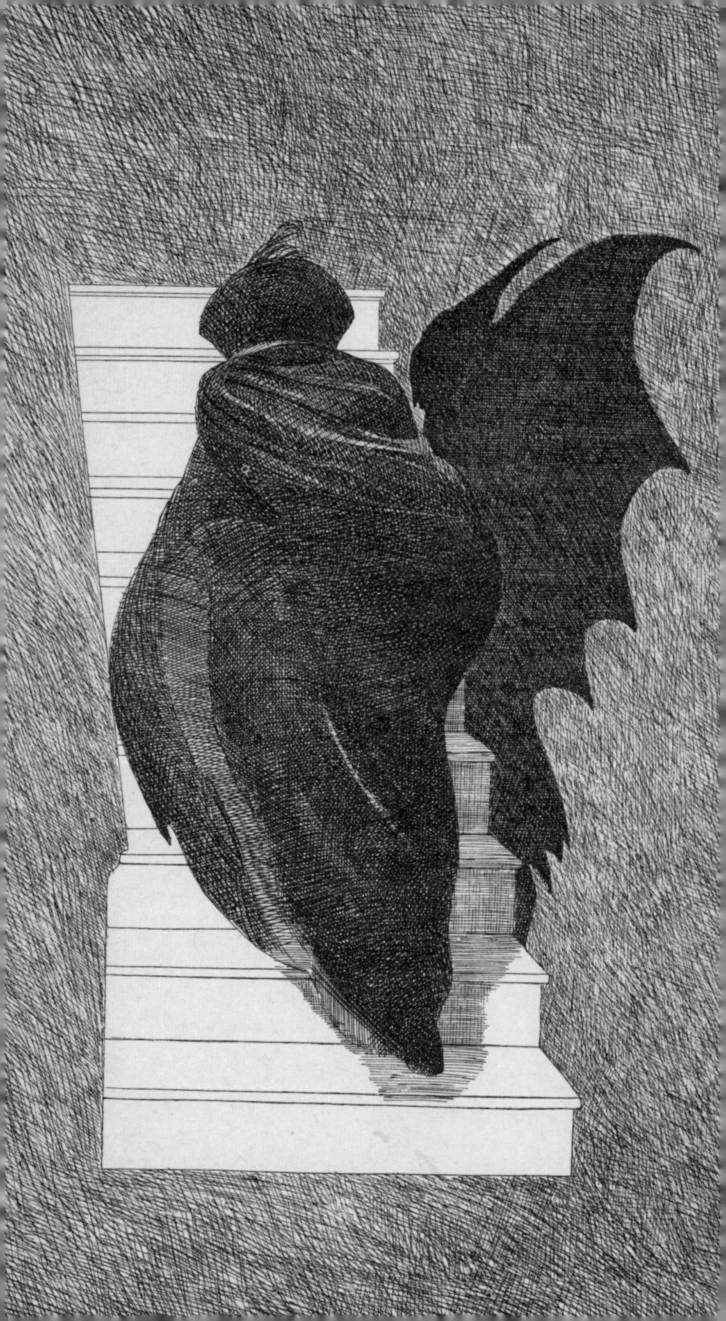

off. I heard a faint click later which told me he had closed his door.

He had picked Room 13. Just across the hall from the one my aunt had given me. Room 12.

I wondered about that.

Then I looked down at the entry again in the guest book. A. R. Claud. Belgrade.

I felt a chill. Belgrade was in Yugoslavia. One of those European countries near Transylvania. Right around where the vampire Count Dracula had lived for hundreds of years.

I kept looking at his name. Then I got a pencil and paper and began moving the letters around. I felt dizzy.

A. R. Claud also spelled Dracula!

CHAPTER

When my aunt came back, I told her about renting the big room facing the front. Number 13.

"His name is Claud," I said. "He said he stayed here before. He even asked for the same room."

"Claud?" she said. "Is he a tall thin man with black hair? Sort of plastered down?"

Right on, I wanted to say. Looks like Dracula. Even his name spells Dracula if you switch the letters around. Out loud I said, "How come he takes the same room?"

She shrugged. "Habit, I guess. Or maybe superstition."

"I thought you stayed away from the number 13 if you were superstitious."

"Well," she said, "not always. Some people don't mind it if they've been lucky with that number."

"What does he do?" I asked. I hoped she really didn't know. I didn't have to know all the news.

"I believe Mr. Claud is an actor. Yes, I'm sure he is."

I wasn't afraid of actors. Only vampires and werewolves.

"Is he with that summer-theater group?" I asked.

She nodded. "Yes, I think so. He's been a guest here several times the past few years during the summer."

"Did you ever see him in one of the plays?"

My aunt shook her head. "I never have the chance. There are always too many things to take care of here. It's a hard job just to keep this place running."

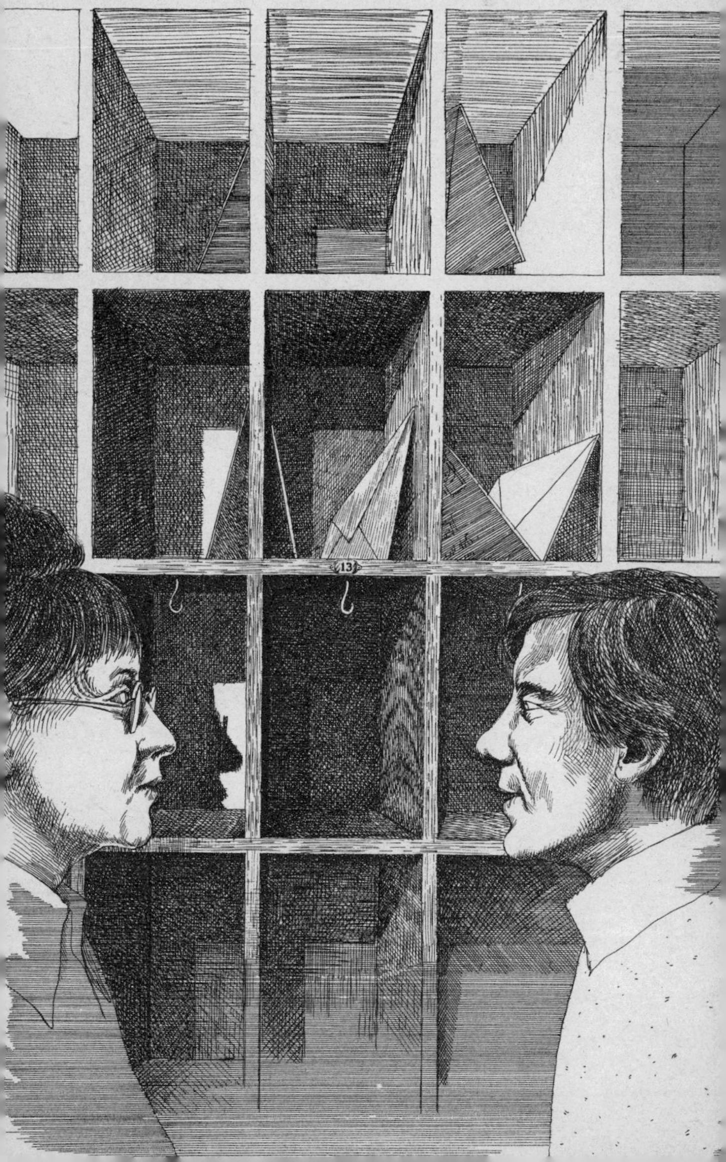
13

"Maybe business will be picking up." I said. "Now maybe some of the other actors will be coming here, too."

Aunt Shirley didn't jump for joy. "That would be nice. But Mr. Claud seems to be the only actor who stays here. The others go to the newer hotel in town. The Crest. It's closer to the summer theater where they work."

Now I felt better about the man upstairs. Being an actor was a good job. And it was nice of him to want to stay at my aunt's hotel.

Maybe he's a good vampire, I thought. Or maybe just a part-time vampire. I wondered if either of those could be possible.

A little later, my aunt called me over. "It's near dinner time, Larry. Perhaps you'd better knock on Mr. Claud's door. Remind him in case he's forgotten when we eat here."

"I told him when he checked in," I said. "He said he knew all about it."

She went back to folding napkins. "Well, all right, then."

When Jill came down, I told her about the

new guest being an actor. Her mouth opened and her eyes got wider.

"Oh, wow! Maybe if I give him terrific service, he'll find a part in a play for me."

I didn't want to alarm her. "Well, yeah. Maybe."

I was kept busy during dinner. All the guests were down at the tables eating except Mr. Claud. My aunt seemed kind of bugged by this.

"Perhaps he forgot, Larry, or fell asleep. I wouldn't want him to miss dinner on his first night back."

"Okay." I went upstairs and knocked on his door. "Dinner, Mr. Claud. It's being served now."

He didn't answer. I tried it again louder.

Nothing.

"Last call for dinner," I said.

I waited there and he didn't answer. He might have fallen asleep. Or maybe he was in the bathroom taking a shower. I took out my passkey and opened the door.

"Mr. Claud," I said. "Dinner time."

The room was empty. The bathroom was empty.

I felt a breeze and saw the curtains move.

I went to the open window. It was nearly dark outside. A big oak stood about five feet away. I didn't see Mr. Claud up in that tree, either.

But he could have gotten out that way. Leaned over and jumped. Grabbed on to one of those thick branches. Then slid down to the ground.

But there was another way he could have done it.

He could have flown right out the window!

CHAPTER

I told my aunt the man wasn't in his room. She looked surprised. "I didn't see him go out," she said.

She had been sitting behind the check-in desk near the stairs. She had a full view of the doorway out.

Maybe vampires moved faster than ordinary people.

I could have asked some of the guests sitting on the front porch if they had seen him walk out. Or jump or fly out the window. But I didn't want to scare away her paying guests.

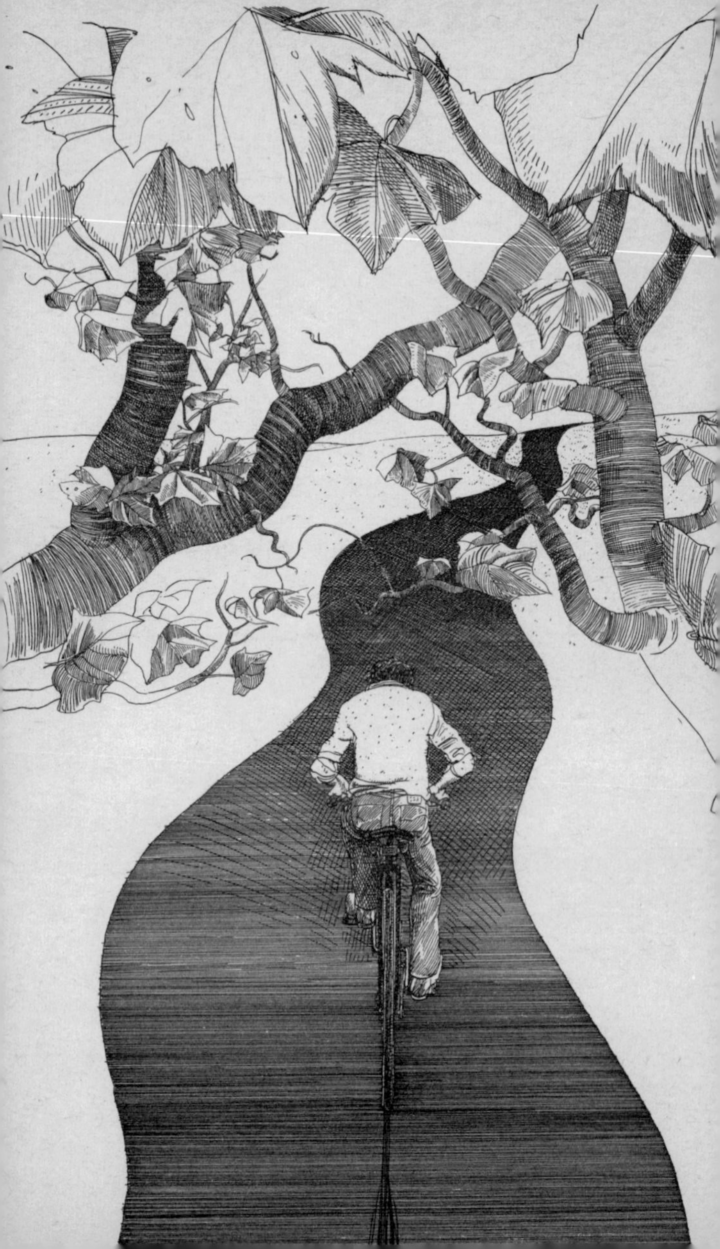

I decided to cool it. Forget how he went out. All I was interested in now was how he was coming back. And when.

After dinner was over, Jill and I played Ping-Pong in the game room. I won one game out of five. Then we played checkers. She won three games straight. Some girls can do those things to you.

Then she said good night and went upstairs. She had to iron her waitress uniform. Her room was on the floor above mine. Room 28.

I watched TV for a while. Then I took a walk outside around the hotel grounds. It was very quiet and the air was still. There were deep dark shadows around the oaks. An owl hooted. The sudden call made me jump.

I wondered what I would do if I saw a giant bat.

I found my uncle's ten-speed bike in the barn. The tires felt okay. I rode it around a little to check it out. All it needed was a little oil on the sprockets. Now I had something to get around on.

The hallway was dimly lit when I went upstairs. No light showing under Mr. Claud's door. I didn't hear him moving around inside. I undressed and went to bed. I tried to keep one ear open to hear him when he got back. Instead I fell sound asleep.

I dreamed that a big black bird was following me. But I hid under some trees and it flew off flapping its wings. It made a sound like a rooster crowing.

I woke up. Dawn was breaking. Chickens were softly clucking. I got out of bed fast. I stepped outside my door and listened. I heard the sound of heavy breathing across the hall. Snoring sounds.

Mr. Claud's door was slightly open.

I pushed it open a little more. He was sleeping soundly on his back. Still wearing his dark suit and white shirt. A long black cape with a red lining. His face was chalk white.

His upper lip was drawn back. He looked happy, almost smiling in his sleep. I saw his white teeth. And in the corner of his mouth, a bright red stain. It could have been ketchup. Or blood.

CHAPTER

I didn't bother waking Mr. Claud up to ask if he cut himself shaving. Or cracked his lip on a tough pizza. I pulled his door back to how I found it. Then I tiptoed back to my room and locked my door.

I tried talking to myself about it. There had to be a lot of ways for a man to have blood on his lip without being a vampire. But the one way left bothered me.

After breakfast was over, and the tables cleared, I asked my aunt if I could take off for the village. No problem, she said. As long as I

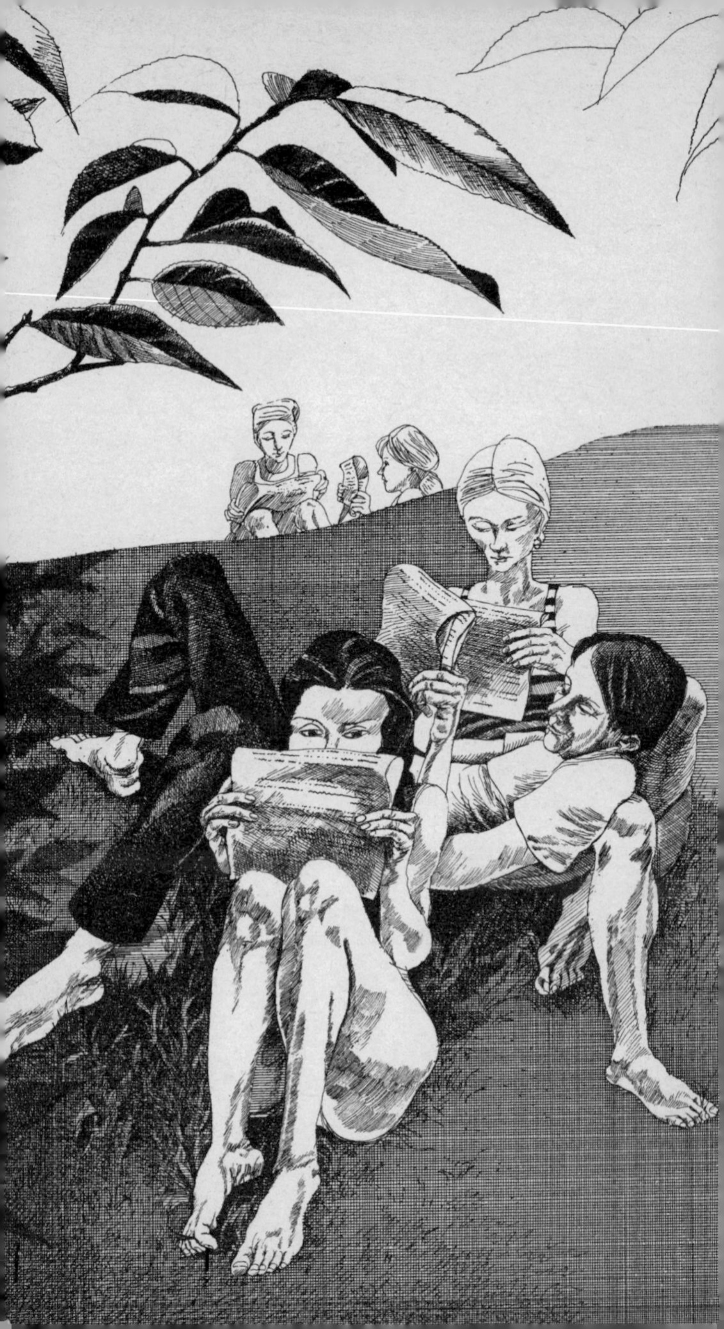

came back in time for lunch. Not to forget my job as busboy.

The blacktop road to the village was about a three-mile ride. My Uncle Bob's bike made good time. At the first gas station, I put some more air in the tires. I asked the gas pump man where the Hammond summer theater actors put on their shows.

It was a short ride out of town. The narrow country road took me to a big red barn. There were shade trees, a few work sheds. Some dusty cars, a panel truck, a couple of vans and campers. It was very peaceful.

The sun was bright and warm. About a dozen people were sitting on the cropped grass or walking around in bare feet. They were reading from blue-bound papers. They had to be actors and actresses talking to themselves out loud and waving their hands.

A fat, balding man was on his knees painting a sign on canvas.

THE HAMMOND PLAYERS in
THE DEAD TELL TALES.

I asked him if A. R. Claud was an actor with this company. He stopped painting, thought about it, and said he didn't think so. I asked if Mr. Claud had acted with them some other time, maybe a few years back.

"This is my first season here," he said. "The man who would know is sitting under that shade tree."

"Who's he?"

"Jack Sail. He's the director."

Mr. Sail kept reading his copy of the play, making notes on the pages. Finally he saw I wasn't going away. I asked him if he could spare a few minutes for some questions.

He frowned. "If you want to join our company, forget it. I hope you didn't run away from home to become an actor."

I told him no, all I was here about was Mr. A. R. Claud. Had he ever acted with these Hammond players?

The director shook his head. "I've been directing this acting group the past five years. Claud, you said? Never heard of him."

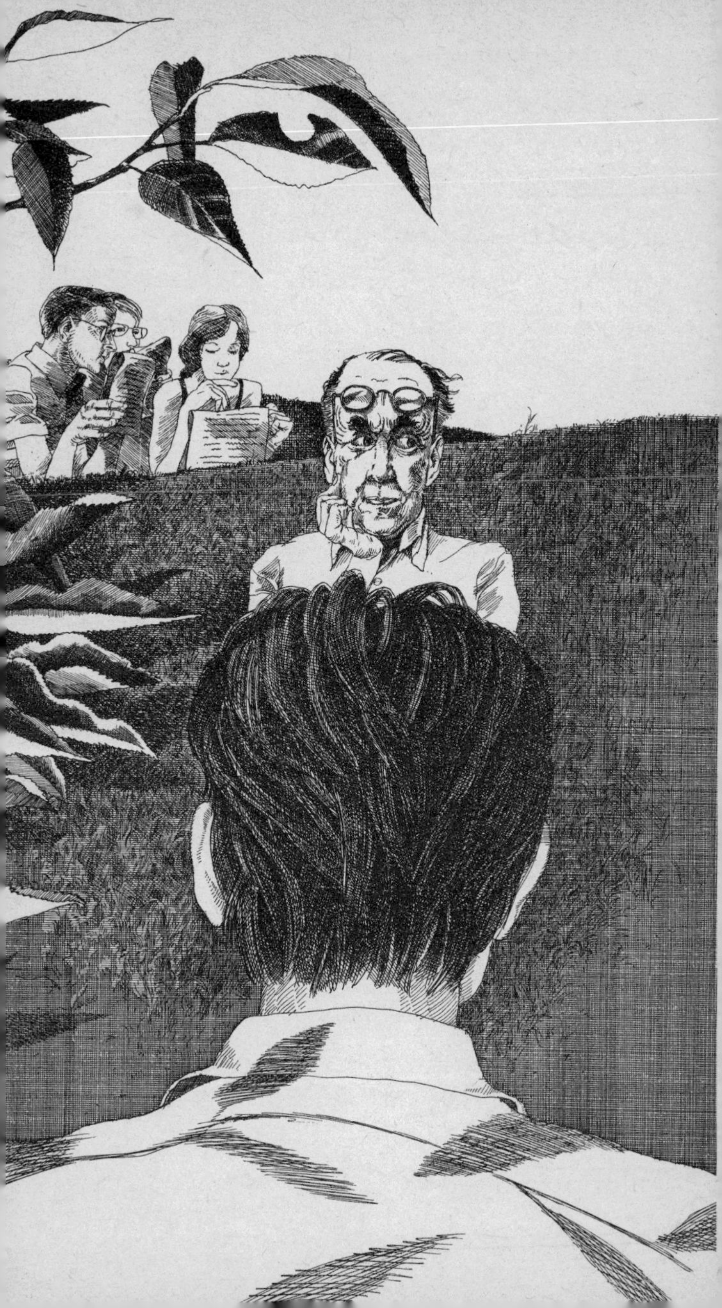

"A tall thin man," I said. "He looks like Dracula."

He put down his script. "That rings a bell," he said. "But you gave me the wrong name. His name isn't Claud. It's Clyde. Andrew Clyde."

"Sorry," I said. "I thought it was Claud. Anyway, what I wanted to know was if he was an actor."

He shook his head at me. He spoke very fast. "Clyde was no actor. He's a magician."

I looked surprised. "With this summer-theater group?"

He sighed heavily. I could tell he wanted to get back to reading his script. "We did a play here a few years ago. Something that called for a real-life magician. Clyde had an act. He also did hypnotism and juggling. I think he tried to be an actor once but couldn't cut it.

"He became an acrobat. Did circus work. Trapeze and high-wire act, I think. He had a bad fall and became a magician. Not a great one, but good enough for what we needed. That answer your question?"

I was thanking him, ready to go.

"The guy always had bad luck, it seems," he said. "The summer he worked for us, there was another accident. His assistant, the girl he worked with, drowned up here on the lake. He couldn't work after that. We cut the play short. I never saw him again."

I thanked him even more. Then I got on my Uncle Bob's bike and pedaled madly back to the hotel.

CHAPTER

There was still time before lunch. My aunt was upstairs cleaning. I dug around below the counter and found the registry books for the past five years.

Mr. Claud was right. He had been coming to this hotel during the summer months starting three years back. Like he said. But he forgot his own name. His neat handwriting was easy to spot.

The first time he wrote: Andrew Clyde. New York City.

Andrew Clyde
New York City

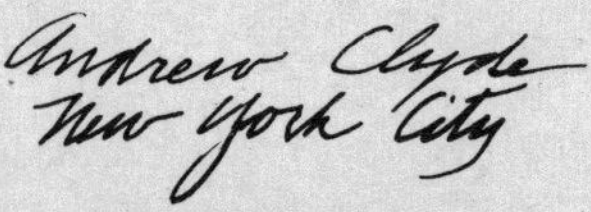

The next year, he wrote: Drew C. Lydell. Miami.

Drew C. Lydell
miami

The next year, he wrote: Claude Dellic. Bucharest.

Claude Dellic
Bucharest

Now he was A. R. Claud. Belgrade.

The first time he spent five weeks at the hotel.

The second time he spent only one week.

The next time he stayed only three days.

I closed the big ledger books and put them back under the counter. I wondered why Mr. Claud had so many names. Also why he came from so many places.

What was he doing in that cemetery? Why did he go around at night dressed up like Dracula? Where did he go?

Had he been eating a hamburger or was that really blood on his lip? If it was blood, whose was it?

(39)

I remembered with a shiver how he whirled around like a cat at the cemetery. The mean look he gave me. The power in his eyes that buckled my knees.

The very next day he checked in at our hotel. Had he followed me there? *Was he after me?*

He wasn't working with the Hammond theater group now. So why was he hanging around here?

Why did he keep coming back to this hotel?

Why did he always want the same room?

Why didn't he eat downstairs with the other guests?

There were other questions. But my aunt was ringing the little bell that told everybody it was time for lunch.

Time for the busboy to get to work.

Jill came up. She looked terrific in her waitress outfit. "How you doing?" she said smiling.

"Great," I lied.

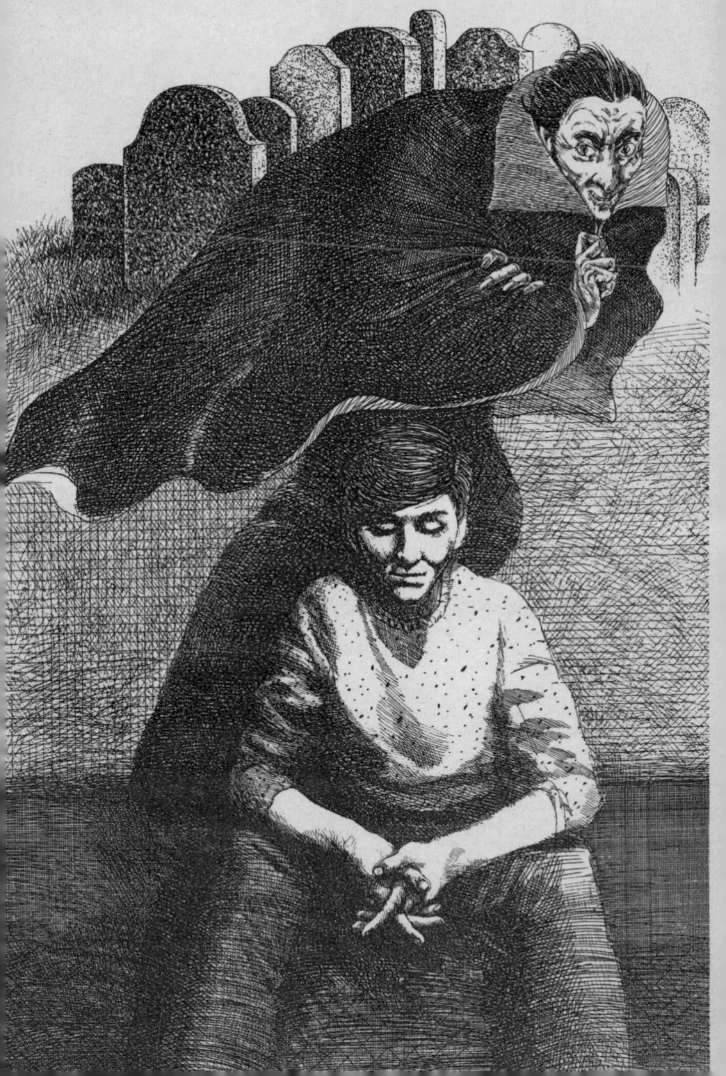

CHAPTER

We served more people for lunch. Not people staying at the hotel but travelers on the road. My aunt had a reputation for serving terrific meals at fair prices.

Jill and I were kept on the run. She asked me to point out the actor. I looked. Mr. Claud was skipping another meal.

I wished I knew more about vampires. How to tell them from other people. The man at the summer playhouse had told me Claud was a magician, and an acrobat. But I had a one-track mind and didn't believe him.

I figured you don't go around telling people you're a vampire. You don't hand out business cards.

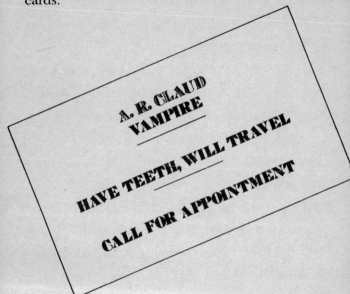

A. R. CLAUD
VAMPIRE

HAVE TEETH, WILL TRAVEL

CALL FOR APPOINTMENT

After lunch I asked my aunt if I could take off. I wanted to look at some books in the library. She was glad I was showing an interest in her home town.

The library, a former church, was in the middle of the village. Made of big stone blocks, it was nice and cool inside. It also had a lot of books.

I found a few on vampires. Mostly folktales. Some history. There really was a Count Dracula once. He killed a lot of people. But he didn't bite them to death. He had his soldiers slay them. He had a bad temper.

The other stories were like the TV movies I had seen. The living dead. Taking the blood of sleeping victims. Flying around like some big bat at night. Back in the coffin to sleep by break of dawn. The only way to get rid of them was to find them asleep and use a pointed wooden stake.

I put the books back on the shelves. Then I saw a newspaper rack in a corner of the library. They had the village newspaper, *The Hammond News*. Daily issues that went back for twenty years.

I didn't have to go back that far.

I turned back three years. A back page had an ad for the Hammond Summer Theater Group. They were rehearsing a new play, *The Devil Inside Us*. To be performed during July and August. Featuring real magic!

Now I had to find some news about a month later.

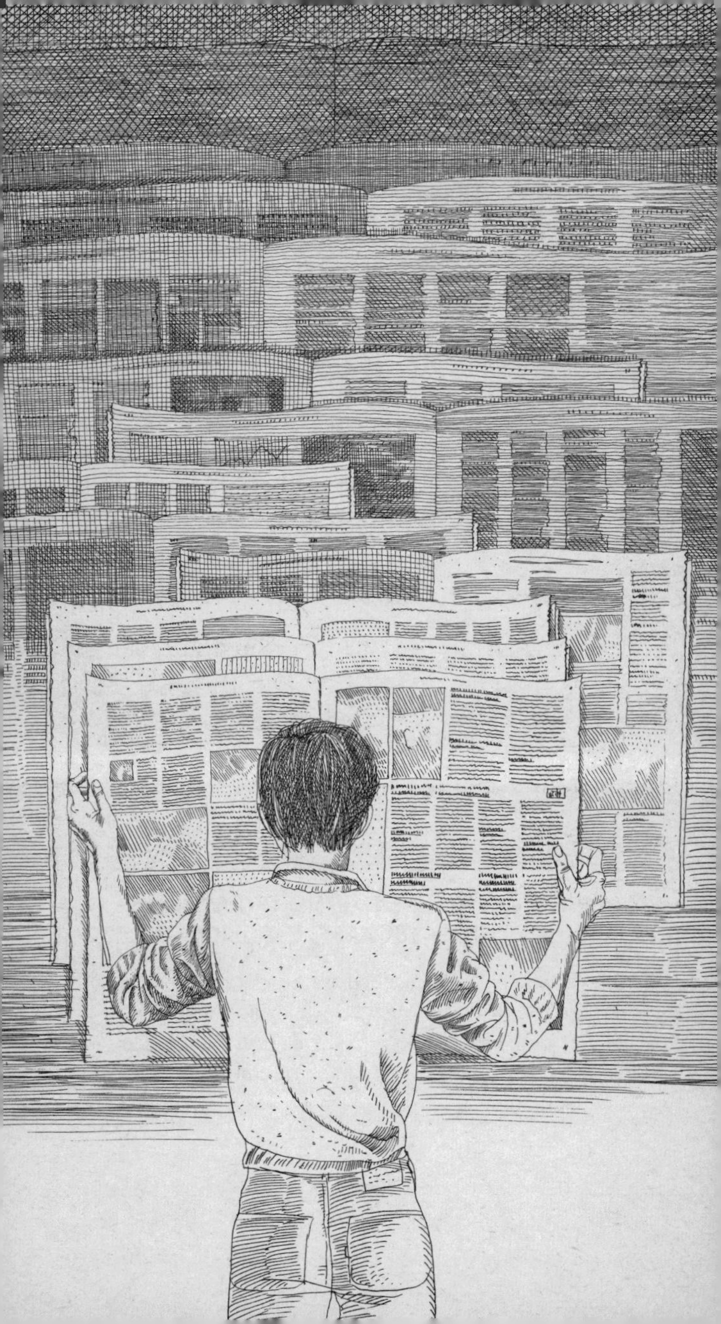

It was on the front page.

TRAGEDY IN LAKE

Maria Palmer, 26, a performer with the local Hammond Theater summer players, was accidentally drowned last night when her canoe overturned. Miss Palmer was assistant to the noted magician Mr. Andrew Clyde, also appearing with the Hammond players. Local police dragged the lake for several hours before recovering her body. She had severe cuts and bruises and it is believed her canoe struck a rock.

Canoes can be tricky. But she must have been going awfully fast to have hit that rock so hard, I thought.

I was putting the old papers back when another headline caught my eye.

SERIES OF SUMMER HOME BURGLARIES CONTINUE TO BAFFLE POLICE

More than a dozen waterfront homes have been looted the past few weeks. Jewelry and valuable silver have been taken. Sheriff Post of Hammond County admits to a lack of clues.

It seemed my aunt was wrong when she told me nothing much ever happened in Hammond.

I left the library and headed my bike back to the hotel. It was late afternoon.

Then I had another idea. I pedaled toward the cemetery instead.

This time I was more careful. There was a grove of trees bordering the graveyard. I parked my bike and sneaked up quietly.

He was there again.

Not standing around this time looking at the tombstones. He was busy. Using a long-handled shovel.

I watched him at it for a while and then left. Now I had something else to wonder about.

Why was Mr. A. R. Claud digging a hole there?

CHAPTER

At dinner Jill stopped me. "Where's that actor you told me about? Doesn't he ever eat?"

"He's tall and thin," I said. "I guess he doesn't eat much."

"Tall and thin? What else does he look like?"

"Like Dracula," I said glumly.

Jill laughed. I looked at her surprised.

"That explains it," she said. "Maybe he's a vampire then, not an actor. He drinks blood after midnight instead of eating meals."

I laughed with her. I had some facts. That Mr. Claud was in the entertainment business. A magician. A former acrobat. Hypnotist. Juggler.

But I didn't trust that stuff. My one-track mind didn't let me believe it.

"Well, remember," I said. "He only looks like Dracula."

"Far out," Jill said merrily. "I still want to meet him. My first chance to meet a real live actor."

I worried about that, too. I knew Jill took acting seriously.

The dining room was nearly full for dinner. We were kept busy and it seemed to take forever. Afterward, we flopped outside on the porch to catch our breath.

"How about some Ping-Pong?" she said.

She won the first three games.

"Checkers?"

She beat me two games straight.

"I'm better at watching TV," I said.

After some of that, she yawned. "I'm pooped. Got to get to bed," she said.

I watched the set a little longer. Keeping one eye open for Mr. Claud coming back from the cemetery.

Finally I gave up and went to my room.

It looked like a hurricane hit it.

My mattress was turned over. The drawers of the chest open, my stuff thrown around. Even the pillowcases were turned inside out.

It had to be Claud. Who else?

Okay, I said to myself, suppose it's Claud. What's he looking for?

I couldn't guess. After I cleaned up my room I was so tired I fell asleep.

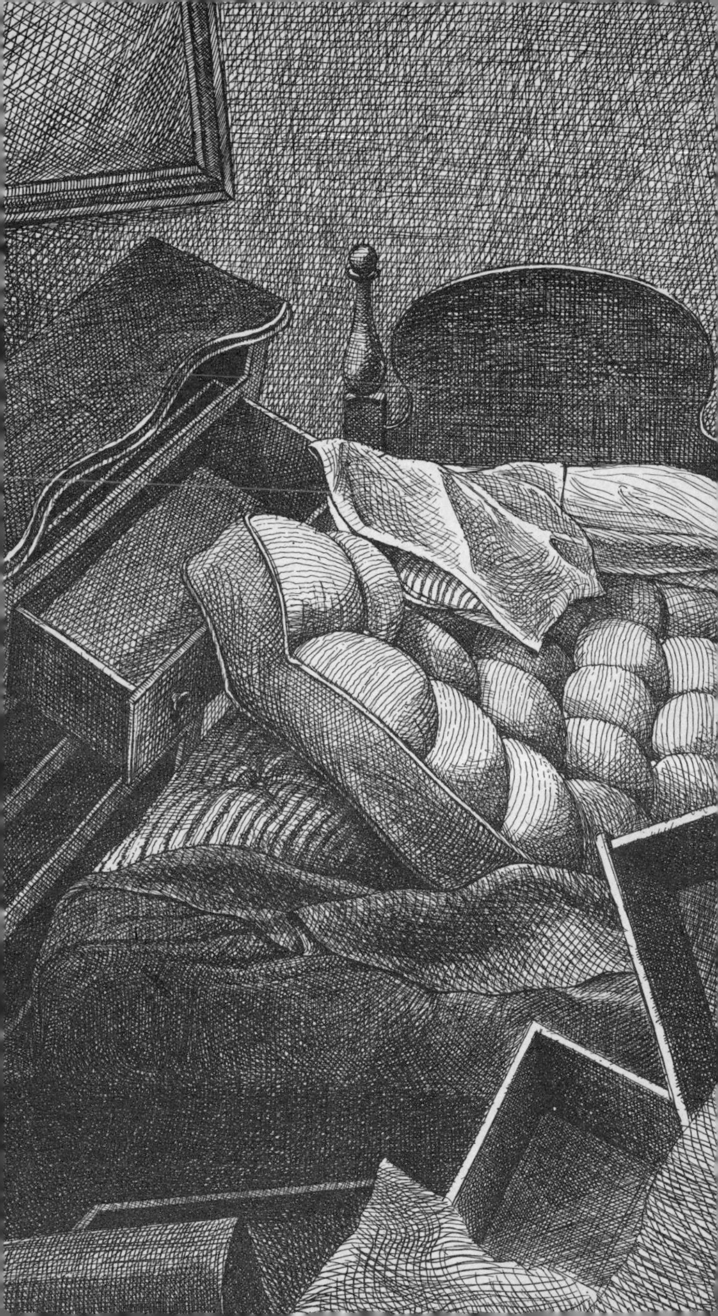

CHAPTER

In my dream, I was running for my life. A big black bird was chasing me. No matter where I turned, it kept on following me.

A strange flapping sound woke me. I sat up in the dark room scared stiff. I felt a breeze and looked toward the window. It was wide open but I couldn't remember opening it that much. Then I sighed, relieved. It was the curtains flapping in the night wind.

There's your big bird, I told myself.

I got up and went to the window. A pale moon lit up the rear sheds and the grounds behind the hotel. The chickens were quiet. Like the rest of the hotel. Everybody sleeping but me.

And maybe Mr. Claud, I thought. It was way after midnight. Time for him to be doing his vampire number.

If he really had one. I still didn't know.

I went to my door. Unlocked it and carefully looked out. The hallway was dark. Nobody out there. I looked across at Room 13. No light under the door. Mr. Claud was asleep, it appeared. Unless he was out again.

I wondered again why he had torn my room apart. What was he looking for?

Slowly I got an idea.

I checked my watch. Two o'clock in the morning. The long hallway seemed to creak with every step I took.

At the steps, I looked down at the counter. The light was dim. The dining room dark. Nobody was around.

I found the big check-in ledgers again. This time I was looking for a special one. His first time.

The handwriting was neat and light. A girl's

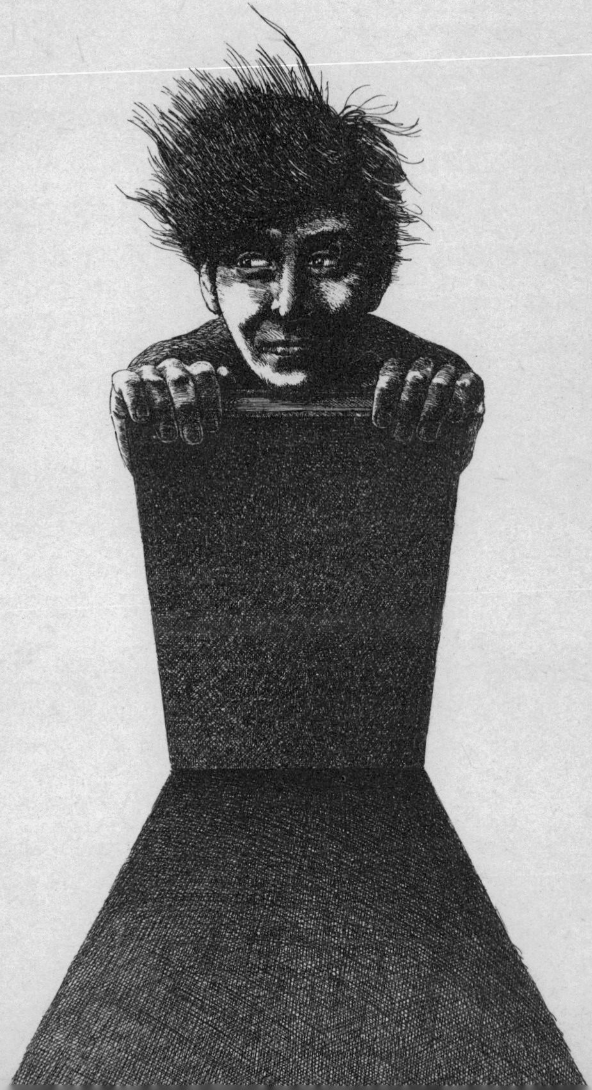

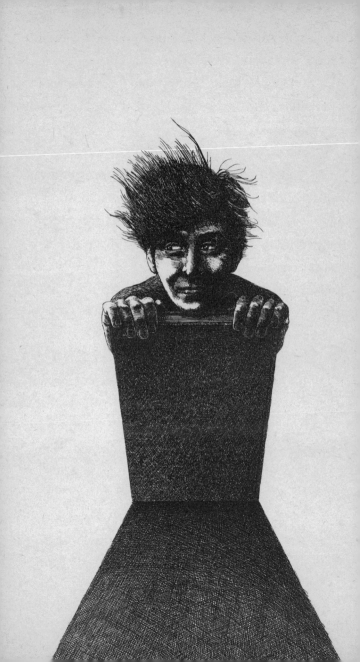

handwriting. Maria Palmer. 313 West 14th Street. New York City.

In the next column was the room she had been given.

Number 12.

Same as mine.

I checked the dates. She had come to the hotel the same time as Andrew Clyde. Now she was dead. Drowned in that canoe accident three years ago.

That still didn't explain why my room was searched. I was about to close the ledger when I felt a chill. The hair rose at the back of my neck. I had goose pimples.

I looked up and there he was.

Pale face white as chalk. Black eyes boring into mine.

Dracula and I—alone.

His voice was soft. Almost like a whisper.

"Well," he said, "have you found what you're looking for?"

I couldn't think of anything to say. He stared at me for a few long seconds. Then his thin lips twisted into a wry smile. I blinked and suddenly he was gone.

I didn't hear him go up the stairs.

Just as I hadn't heard him come down.

I waited a while until I got my breath back. And some courage.

Then I went upstairs again. Holding one hand to my throat while feeling very foolish about it.

Nobody bit me. There wasn't any big black bird waiting on my bed.

I locked my door and pulled down the window. When I got into bed, I was cold all over.

It took me a long time to fall asleep.

CHAPTER

Breakfast was a mess. I dropped three dishes before getting them to the kitchen sink. When I cleaned up the floor, I saw my hands were shaking. "Don't drop any more dishes," I told them, "or we're out of a job."

Seeing Jill was what gave me the shakes. She had a white Band-aid on her neck.

He got her, I said to myself. Bit her on the neck—like all vampires do.

"What happened to your neck?" I asked.

She shrugged. Put her hand on it. "I guess some little night bug bit me."

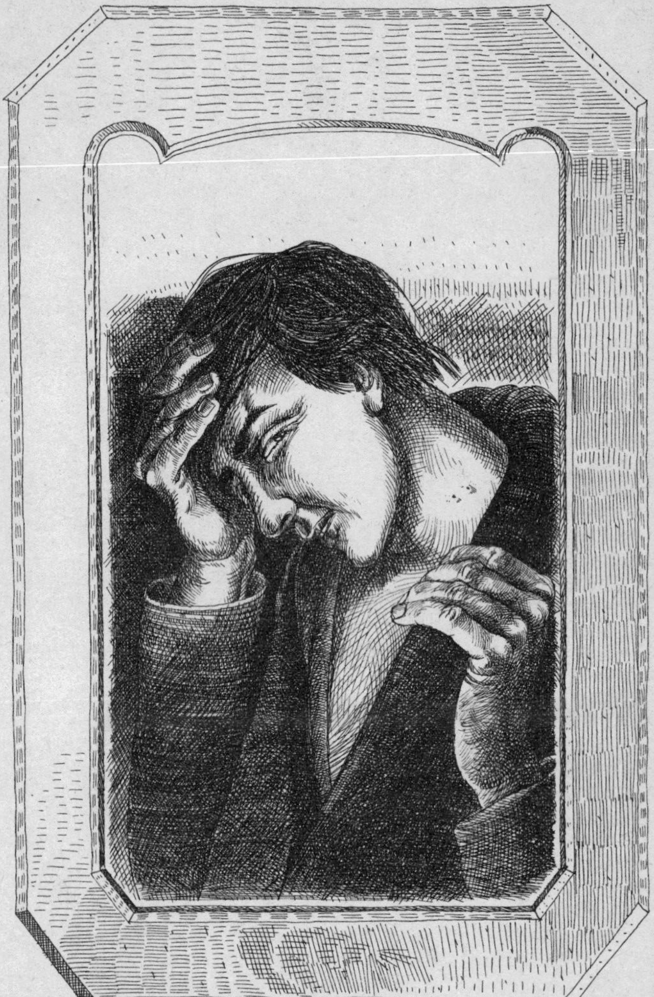

"You guess? Don't you know for sure?"

"How can I tell? I was sleeping."

"Maybe you ought to close your window," I said.

She was peering closely at me. She smiled. "You have the same marks yourself, Larry."

My hand flew to my neck. My voice was hoarse. "I do?"

She nodded. "You've got two tiny little holes. Just like mine. I guess they have a lot of night insects up here."

I picked up my tray and hurried to the kitchen to look in the mirror. On my way there, I dropped the dishes.

The cook looked at me. "Sorry about that," I said.

I looked at my neck in the mirror. There were two little red spots an inch apart. Bug bites?

Vampire bites?

I didn't know what real vampire bites were like. Mr. Claud had white teeth. I couldn't remember if they were pointed.

The spots didn't hurt. I didn't feel weak. If he took my blood, I would feel weak, wouldn't I?

I felt my body. Now that I thought about it, I didn't feel all that great.

I knew one thing for sure.

I was scared stiff.

The sheriff of Hammond County was a medium-sized, chunky man. He liked to squint his eyes and he chuckled a lot. He worked in a small white building at the end of the village. It wasn't a very big police department. I could see only two other men there behind desks.

I told him I was a new visitor to Hammond and working for my aunt up at The Oaks Hotel. Then I asked him if he could tell me anything about the robberies I had read about. If they had ever found the jewels and valuables, or the crooks, or anything else.

"Robberies? What robberies?" he demanded. "We've got a nice peaceful, law-abiding community here."

"About three or four years ago," I said. "During the summer."

He squinted and stopped chuckling. "Well,

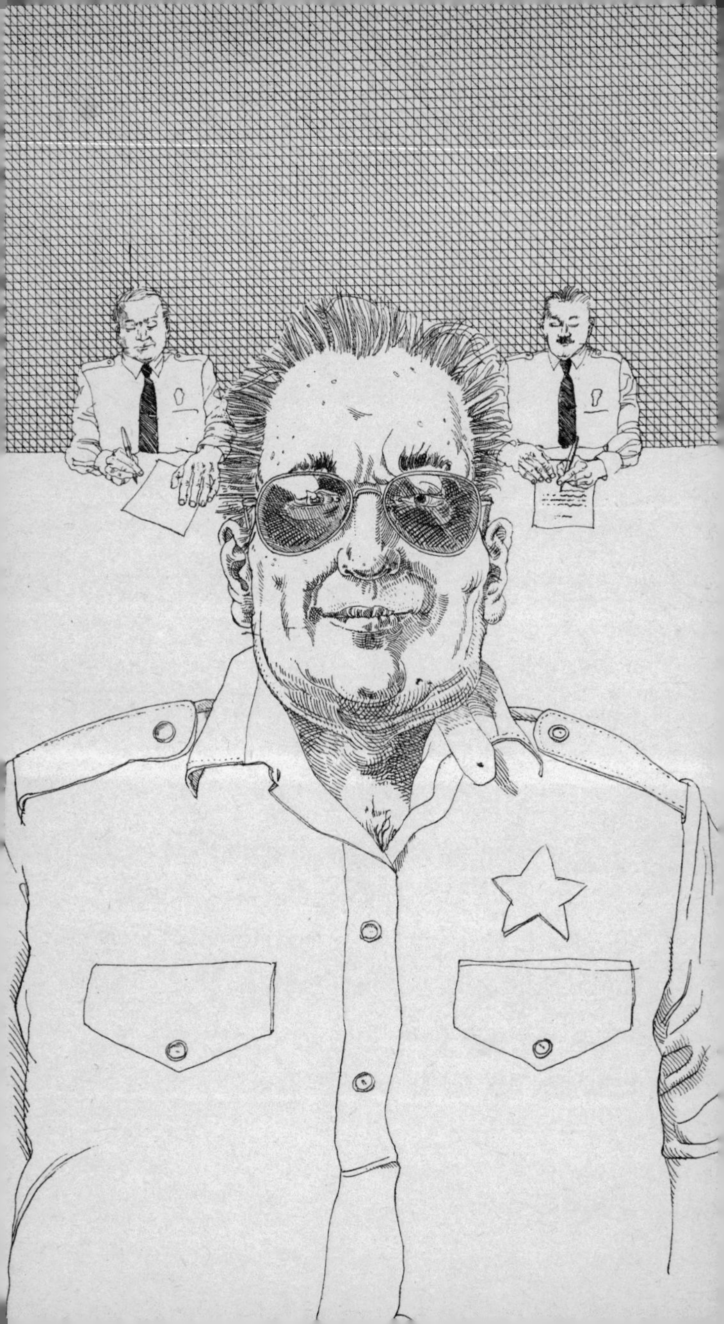

yes, come to think of it. That was quite a thing. Whoever did the jobs did it nice and clean. No, we never did find the haul. Never caught up with whoever planned and did the jobs, either."

I got an idea who did it, I wanted to say. The sheriff leaned toward me, scowling. "How come you're so interested, young fellow?"

I told him it was for a school project. I was going to be a crime reporter someday.

He leaned back and clasped his ample belly. "Well, that's nice, son. Too bad you can't help me on this case. The trail has run kind of cold by now."

I asked him what about the accidental drowning of the young girl who worked in the summer theater.

"What about it?" he asked.

"Are you sure it was accidental?"

He chuckled. "I remember checking that one out myself. Ran her canoe onto a rock, that young lady did. She hit her head and drowned. Not the first one to do it in these parts, either. We average a couple bodies a season. Plain carelessness, is all. And most of 'em don't know how to swim a lick."

I think I know how that happened, I wanted to say. It probably wasn't any accident at all.

But I didn't say it.

The sheriff rustled some papers on his desk. He was getting a little bored with the new crime reporter. "Anything else troubling you, son?"

I got up. I wanted to ask him if they had had any vampires in Hammond before I got there. But I knew that would be one question too much for the sheriff. So I just thanked him and left.

On the way back, my neck began to hurt a little. So instead of heading right back to the hotel, I turned off at the cemetery.

I was very careful to look around the area first. Mr. Claud wasn't anywhere in sight. I went over the low stone wall and right to the spot where I had seen him last. When he was digging around.

He had dug a lot of small holes in many different places. Some of them near tombstones. There was one that gave me the shivers.

It was a big shallow hole. More than a hole, to tell the truth. It looked big enough to be a grave.

I walked around it, looking down at it, feeling dizzy.

It was my exact size!

CHAPTER

It began to rain. That's good, I thought. He wouldn't want to bury me in my grave with all that water. I might float away.

Thinking about vampires and dying can make a person very depressed.

I came back to the hotel from the rear. I looked up at my window. The second floor near the end. How could he get up there from the outside? I wondered. He would have to either swing down on a rope from the pitched roof, or climb up the drainpipe at the end of the building.

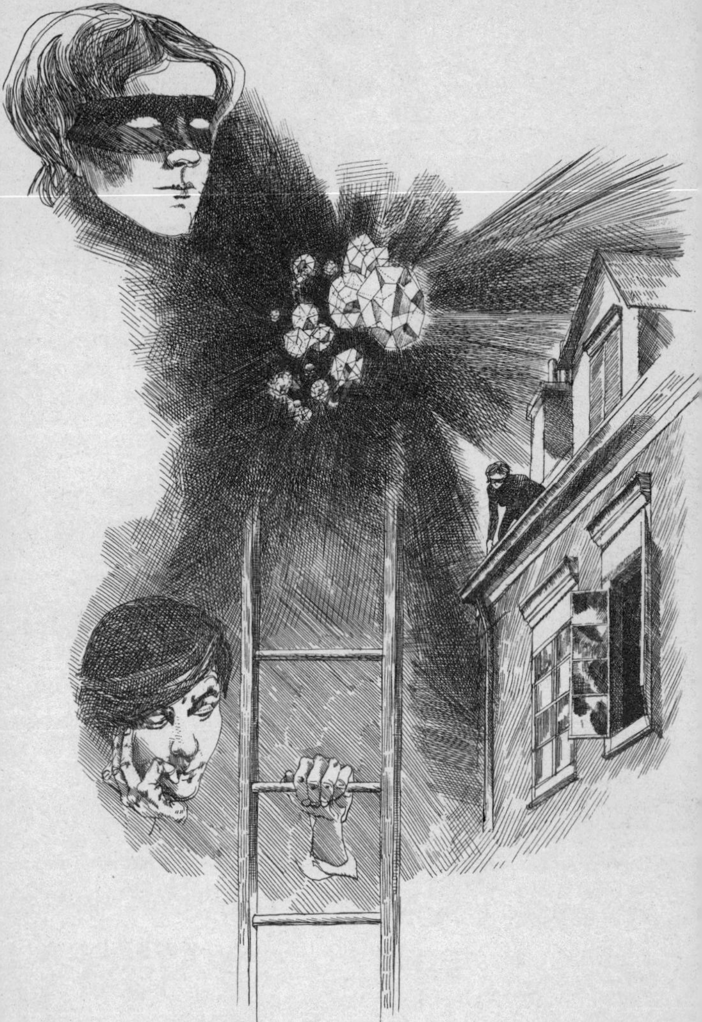

I watched the water spilling out of the gutters of the drainpipe running all around the hotel. Probably clogged up from all those oak leaves, I thought. Maybe I would do my aunt a favor and get up there with a long ladder and clean them out for her.

Suddenly I remembered Mr. Claud wasn't any ordinary man, even if he wasn't a vampire. He had been an acrobat with the circus. Acrobats could do amazing things.

I went over closer to the drainpipe. It was thin and wet and shook a little when I tested it. I wouldn't want to climb up it.

But then I wasn't a man desperately in search of something.

Like the jewels, I thought. The girl was his partner in the robberies. She hid the stuff and wouldn't tell him where.

Okay, maybe, I said to myself. So why is he digging all those holes in the graveyard?

Same answer, I told myself. He doesn't know where Maria hid the stuff. He's got to look all over. That's why he comes back here every year. To look for the jewels.

Hey, that's neat, I told myself. You solved the whole thing. What are you going to do now?

Try to stay alive tonight, I said to myself. If I can live through tonight, I bet I can prove it all.

CHAPTER 14

The afternoon dragged along. Business was off because of the rain. Mr. Claud didn't come down for either lunch or dinner. I rubbed my neck. Well, he didn't have to eat if he got enough blood.

After dinner, Jill and I did the same routine. She was getting better. She beat me five straight in Ping-Pong. Three in a row at checkers.

"Are you sure you're trying?" she said, sighing.

"Sure I'm trying," I said. "You just happen to be pretty good."

"I wish you'd introduce me to that Mr. Claud," she said. "I'd like to tell him what a good actress I am."

"He's in and out," I said. "Meanwhile remember to lock your door and window tonight."

"Why?" she said.

I touched my neck. "You might get bit again."

After some TV, she went up to her room again. It had stopped raining. I went up to my room. I'm too young to die, I told myself. I've got to do something about this.

That's why, an hour before midnight, I grabbed a flashlight and went back to the graveyard.

I checked my watch. If he was a vampire, he was still asleep in his coffin in the crypt. I had till midnight.

If he was only a magician trying to scare me, he was doing a good job of that, too.

I sneaked past the long rows of tombstones. I didn't bother looking at my new grave. I was scared enough without that.

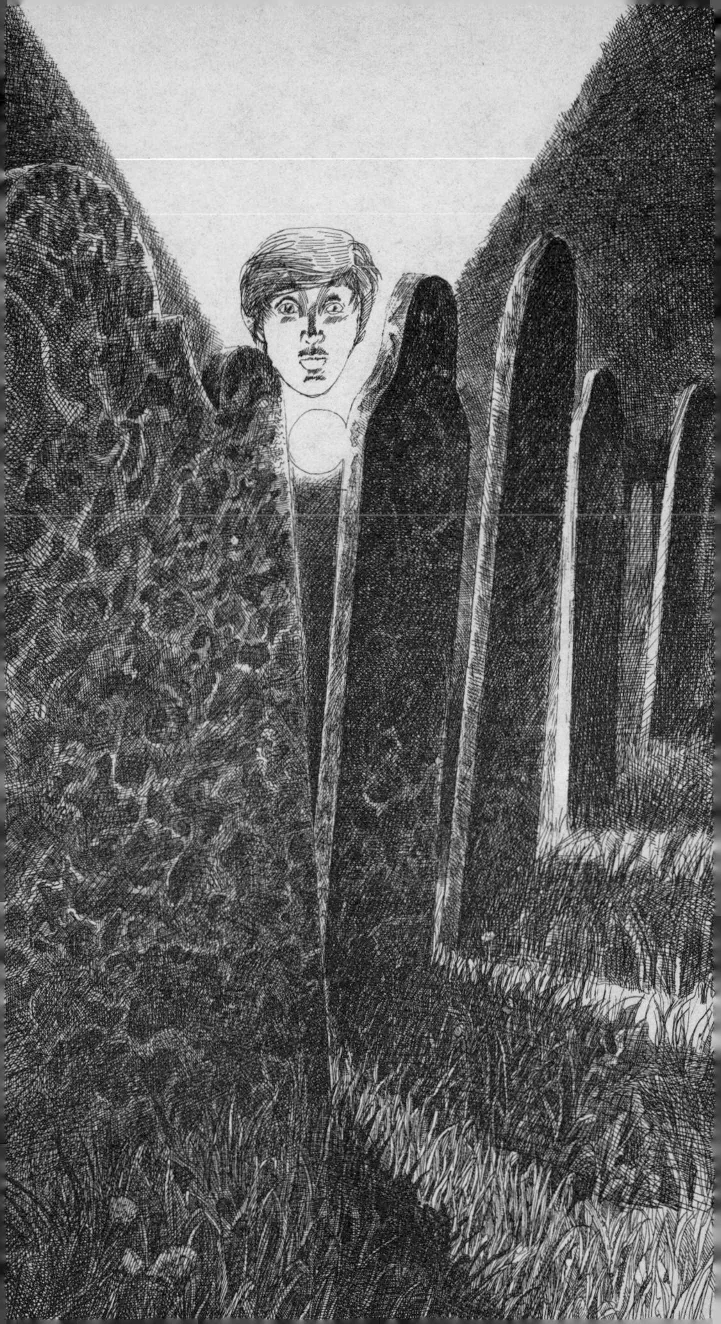

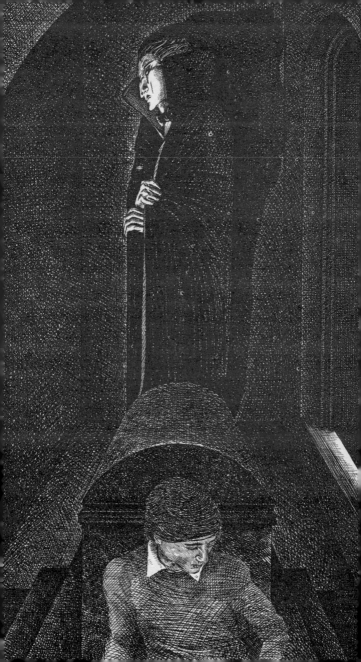

I was breathing hard and sweating under the chill night wind when I reached the marble vault at the end.

The heavy door creaked when I pulled it open. It was dark and spooky inside and I flicked on my pencil flashlight. It showed me where steps were leading to the underground chamber.

Come on, I said to myself, you're not going down there, are you?

I hesitated. Hoping I'd get enough courage to say yes.

Then I froze. I heard a noise from below. It sounded like something I didn't want to believe. Like the dull thud of a coffin closing. *Thunk*. Like that.

Wait here, I told myself. Don't be any dumber than you have to be.

I snapped off my flashlight. Backed up, shivering. I heard soft rustling sounds.

I felt his presence before I saw him. Something very big, blacker than the darkness of the tomb. It came close enough to brush me and I shrank back.

Then there was the creak of the heavy door as it opened. I saw him clearly now framed against the night sky.

A. R. Claud. Wearing a long black cape.

His face was very white. His eyes were black. Blazing. He looked mad enough to bite anybody in half.

Then he was out the door. The long cape streaming behind him.

I took a couple of deep breaths. Then I went to the door and slowly poked it open.

Only a few seconds had passed, but I couldn't see him anywhere.

I heard a strange and eerie cry and shivered. I looked up toward the cry.

It looked like a bird. A very big black bird.

It was flying toward the hotel.

Come on, I told myself. *You've got to get there first.*

CHAPTER

I was running. But I didn't know why. I didn't have any plan. There was no way I saw myself fighting off a vampire.

But I wasn't sure of that, either. No more than I was sure Mr. Claud was a jewel thief.

I got to the hotel breathing hard. Wondering what I was going to do. How it was all going to end.

The hotel was dark. After midnight, everybody was asleep. I came along the back way looking up at the dark windows. The moon was over my shoulder. I saw a long dark shadow in front

of me. It moved when I did. I was frightened until I realized it was my own shadow.

I looked up for the big black bird, a vampire,
or A. R. Claud. I didn't see any of them. It began
to rain again.

I went around to the front of the hotel. Hoping to see a light in Mr. Claud's room. Then I
would be sure he wasn't flying around looking for
somebody to bite. There wasn't any light.

I heard a loud scream. A girl's voice. It had
to be Jill.

Now I knew why I had to get back to the
hotel first. *Dracula was after Jill!* In all the TV
movies, it was the women he would bite. Making
them his slaves!

I took the hotel steps two at a time. She let
out another bloodcurdling yell. People were stir-
ring around. Putting on their lights. Opening
their doors. All they saw was me running like
mad.

I raced down the third-floor hallway. I was
almost at her door when she came running out.
"What's happening?" I said.

She had trouble talking. Finally she got it

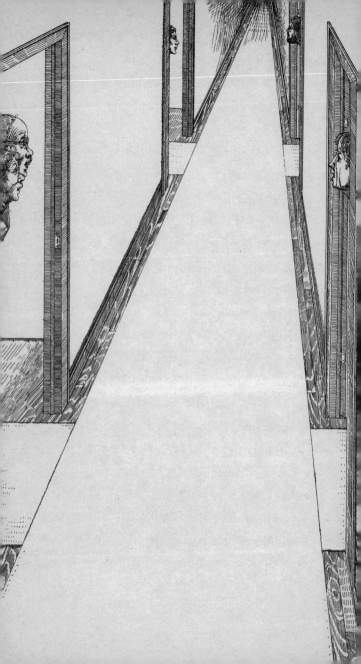

out. "Some kind of giant bat or something. Outside my window!"

Her light was on. I couldn't see anything out the window. She let out another yelp, pointing. "There it is!"

I looked but still couldn't see anything. Just rain running down the glass pane. I went closer, staring out.

When it came by, I nearly jumped out of my sneakers. It came flying in from the side. A huge dark shape. It was him—Dracula—upside down—flying!

He came close to the window. He hovered there a long second. His mouth opened. He had sharp white teeth. His hands beat at the wet glass.

Like a bird, I thought. Like a vampire bat. *What is he?*

Then as suddenly, he was gone. Jill yelled in my ear. "What is it? Is that a man or what? What's he doing out there?"

The rain gusted wet in my face as I lifted her window. He had dropped to my window now.

He swung from side to side. White hands reaching out.

Suddenly I heard a cracking noise overhead. Bricks and stones began falling down. The dark figure dangling below looked up. His pale face now looked frightened.

More stones poured down. He pushed himself away from my window and flung himself to the side of the house. He grabbed at the drainpipe. His legs were thrashing as he tried to right himself.

I saw the thin rope tied around his body then. He must have tied it to the chimney on the roof. A neat way to fly!

He was still struggling to get right side up when there was another tearing, cracking sound and the drainpipe began to give way. Then, almost in slow motion, it fell away from the building.

Dracula screamed.

His scream was stopped by an awful crunch when he hit the ground. His leg was twisted under him. More bricks and stones rained down.

Then the whole rain gutter tore away from the building and fell on him. He didn't move.

"Come on," I yelled to Jill. "I'm calling the sheriff."

"The sheriff?" she said. "Why not the hospital?"

CHAPTER 16

My aunt stood shaking her head in the rain. "Oh, the poor man. What happened?"

I was trying to lift the drainpipe off him. It broke at the joint with the gutter. A leather sack fell out.

"What's that?" Jill said.

I opened the strings and shook some of it out in my hand. "That's why I called the sheriff. All these diamond rings and bracelets and stuff."

Jill stared. "What about them? And what were they doing in your aunt's drainpipe?"

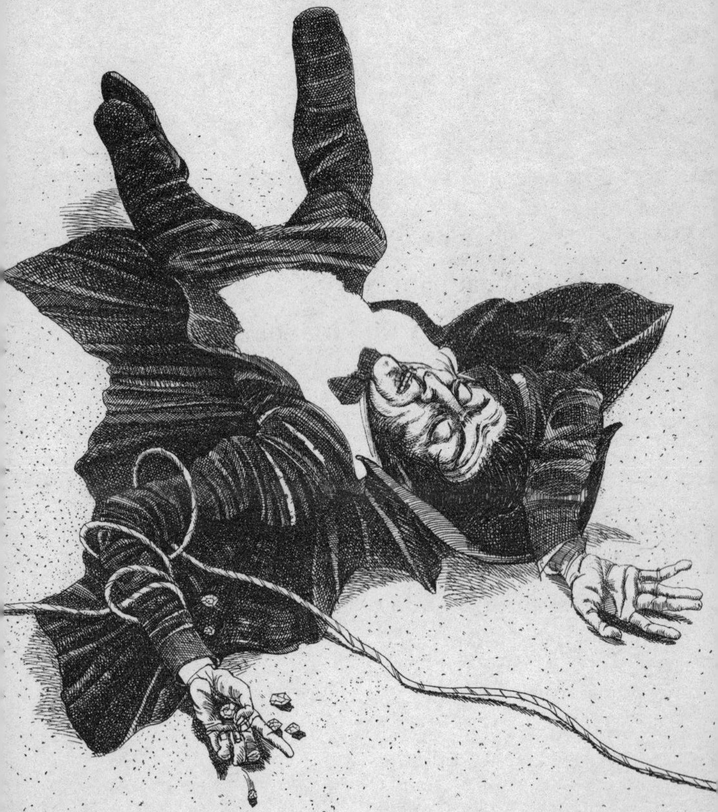

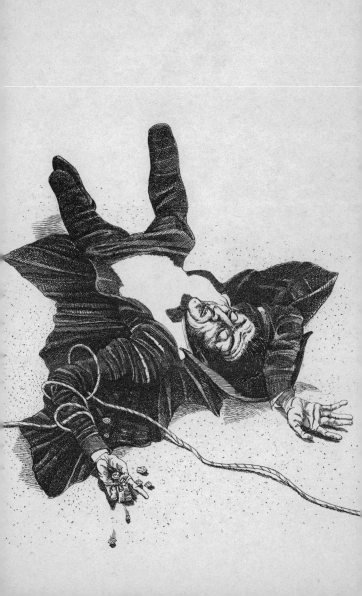

I pointed to the man lying there on the wet ground. "He helped steal them but he didn't know they were hidden up there. That's why he's here. To find the missing loot. He only pretended to be Dracula to scare me."

She began laughing. "Dracula? You really thought he was Dracula?"

"Well, not really," I said.

You can't tell people everything.

Sheriff Post looked me over. "Stole them jewels, you say? Maybe killed the girl on the lake?"

"That's right, sheriff," I said.

The ambulance had come and taken Mr. Claud away. The sheriff didn't look too happy about being called out of bed after midnight.

"I hope you got some proof, son," he said.

I told him all that had happened from the time I got to Hammond.

"Okay," he said. "So this fellow Claud was digging around in the graveyard. Walking around the crypt. You ever see him take anything?"

"Well, no, not exactly," I said.

"What about that other stuff?" he said. "The murder and all."

"Well, I figured it all out, sheriff," I said. "Everything checks out, just like it happened."

The sheriff forgot how to chuckle. "You figured it out?"

"If you check with the theater director, he'll tell you Mr. Claud worked there then as Andrew Clyde. He and the girl had only a small part in the play. He had a lot of time to rob those houses. He only tried to scare me pretending he was Dracula," I said. "So he could get at the jewels Maria Palmer hid."

He looked up at the roof. The old chimney was half gone now. "The bag was in the gutter and drainpipe, you say," he said. "How do you figure they got up there?"

I shrugged. "I guess she just threw them up there. Trying to hide them from him."

"Not bad," the sheriff said. "Only guessing doesn't count."

"He only had that small part in the play that year," I said. "While all the other actors were working, he and the girl took off for the other

(84)

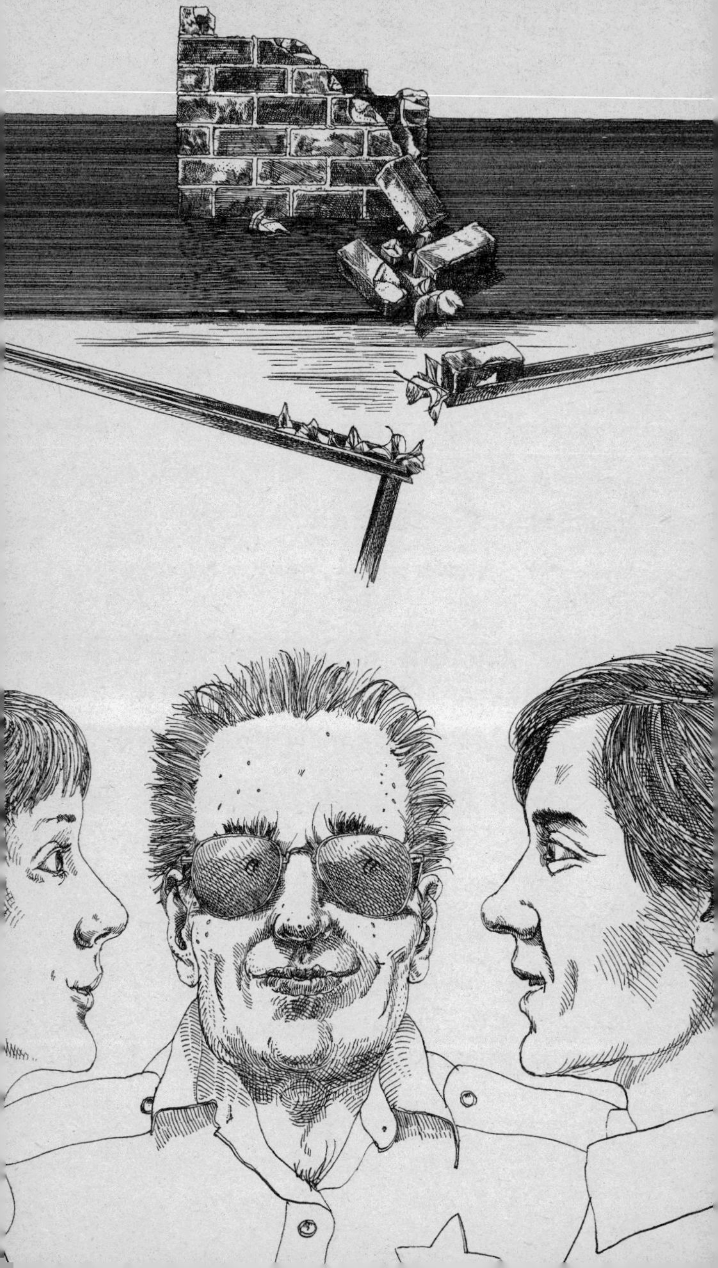

side of the lake. All the rich homeowners were away. Over here to see the summer players."

"Sure," he said. "That's possible, too. But can you prove any of it?"

"Well, no, but . . ."

The sheriff sighed. "It's all up to Mr. Claud now. He'll have to confess before we can arrest him."

"Do you think he'll do that?" I said.

"Don't think he's crazy enough to do that," the sheriff said. "Like I said, there's no proof against him. No witnesses."

"But the jewels," I said. "It's all there, isn't it?"

He chuckled. "Sure enough. But according to the evidence, Claud didn't find them. *You* did."

"What about all those different names he used?"

"Ain't no law against a man changing his name. Providing he hasn't done anything wrong."

"You mean, you can't charge him with any-thing?"

"Well, not exactly. I reckon we can hold him accountable for pulling down your aunt's chimney and drainpipe."

The sheriff left after that. Taking the bag of jewels. He said there was a good chance I might get a reward. It would take a while, he added, until they figured out what belonged to each party.

"About how long?" I said.

"Well, if you still got this summer job next year, drop in, son. I might have some news for you."

I never found out what happened to A. R. Claud, alias Andrew Clyde, alias the man who looked like Dracula.

I guess after his leg got better, he went home. The bugs kept right on biting my neck and everywhere else the rest of the summer.